W9-CRB-957

SHORT TALES
GREEK MYTHS

HERCULES

Adapted by Shannon Eric Denton
Illustrated by Andy Kuhn

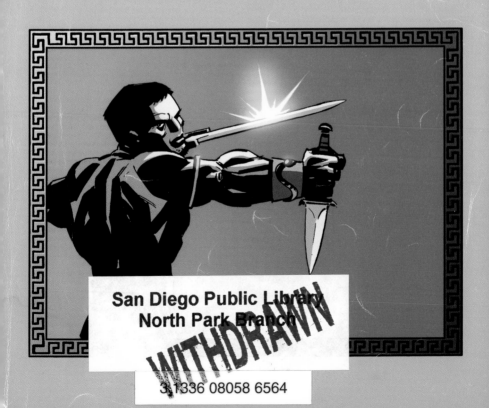

GREEN LEVEL
- Familiar topics
- Frequently used words
- Repeating language patterns

BLUE LEVEL
- New ideas introduced
- Larger vocabulary
- Variety of language patterns

PINK LEVEL
- More complex ideas
- Extended vocabulary
- Expanded sentence structures

To learn more about Short Tales leveling, go to www.abdopublishing.com

Published by Magic Wagon, a division of the ABDO Publishing Group, 8000 West 78th Street, Edina, Minnesota, 55439. Copyright © 2008 by Abdo Consulting Group, Inc. International copyrights reserved in all countries. All rights reserved. No part of this book may be reproduced in any form without written permission from the publisher. Short Tales ™ is a trademark and logo of Magic Wagon.

Printed in the United States.

Adapted Text by ShannonEric Denton
Illustrations by Andy Kuhn
Colors by Wes Hartman
Edited by Stephanie Hedlund
Interior Layout by Kristen Fitzner Denton
Book Design and Packaging by Shannon Eric Denton

Library of Congress Cataloging-in-Publication Data
Denton, Shannon Eric.
 Hercules / adapted by Shannon Eric Denton ; illustrated by Andy Kuhn.
    p. cm. -- (Short tales. Greek myths)
  ISBN 978-1-60270-135-9
 1. Heracles (Greek mythology)--Juvenile literature. I. Kuhn, Andy. II. Title.
 BL820.H5D46 2008
 398.20938'02--dc22

                              2007036067

THE GREEK GODS

ZEUS:
Ruler of Gods
& Men

ATHENA:
Goddess of
Wisdom

HEPHAESTUS:
God of Fire
& Metalworking

HERA:
Goddess of Marriage
Queen of the Gods

HERMES:
Messenger of
the Gods

HESTIA:
Goddess of the
Hearth & Home

POSEIDON:
God of the Sea

APHRODITE:
Goddess of Love

ARES:
God of War

ARTEMIS:
Goddess of
the Hunt

APOLLO:
God of the Sun

HADES:
God of the
Underworld

Mythical Beginnings

Hercules was the son of Zeus and an Earth woman. From an early age, he was incredibly strong.

Zeus's wife Hera hated Hercules and used her powers to make him go insane. While under her spell, Hercules did some terrible things. But, he eventually regained his senses.

When he realized what he had done, he asked for forgiveness. He was told there was a way to make this happen.

In Mycenae, Hercules was forced to serve King Eurystheus.
The king assigned the mighty warrior 10 Labors. The tasks
were so difficult they seemed impossible.

First, Hercules set out to best the Nemean Lion. This beast
terrorized the hills around Nemea.

No arrow could pierce its hide. Hercules would have to find
some other way to beat the lion.

Hercules tracked the lion to a cave that had two entrances.
He blocked one entrance. He then charged into the other.
Hercules caught the great beast off guard but dropped his club.

All Hercules had left was his mighty strength. So, he wrestled
the beast to the ground and defeated it.

His first Labor was complete.

His second Labor was to defeat the nine-headed Lernean
Hydra.

The Hydra was a monstrous serpent. Its nine heads
attacked with venom. And one of the heads could not
be killed.

Hercules took his nephew Iolaus to find this great beast.

They discovered the Hydra's lair. They wanted to lure the massive beast from the safety of its den. So, they shot flaming arrows at it.

Once the Hydra appeared, Hercules attacked with his club. The Hydra wound one of its coils around Hercules's foot. It was impossible for the hero to escape.

Hercules continued to swing his club. But as soon as he smashed one head, two more would burst forth in its place! Luckily, Iolaus was there to help Hercules.

They fought together to defeat the Hydra. As Hercules severed a head, Iolaus torched the neck.

The flames prevented the growth of more heads. Finally, Hercules had the better of the beast.

Once they had removed the mortal heads, Hercules chopped off the immortal head.

Hercules buried this head at the side of the road. Then, he covered it with a gigantic rock.

Hercules returned to Mycenea. Eurystheus ordered Hercules to get the Hind of Ceryneia as the third Labor.

This Hind was a special red deer. It had golden horns and hoofs of bronze. It was the special pet of the goddess of hunting, Diana.

Hercules knew he had to be careful in capturing the Hind.

For an entire year, Hercules tried to catch the Hind. One day, he saw it near a stream. Hercules shot it in the leg so he could catch it.

Diana suddenly appeared and was very angry with Hercules. Hercules explained that he had to catch the deer to complete his third Labor.

Thankful for his apology, Diana healed the Hind. She allowed Hercules to take it to Mycenea and complete his third Labor.

For the fourth Labor, Eurystheus ordered Hercules to bring
him the monstrous Erymanthian boar alive.

Hercules waited until the boar came down the mountain.
Then, he chased it round and round, shouting as loud as he
could.

The boar became worn out from all the running. So Hercules
trapped it in a net and carried it all the way to Mycenae.

He had completed his fourth Labor.

For the fifth Labor, Hercules was ordered to clean King Augeas's stables in one day.

Thousands of animals were brought to the stables every day. The shepherds knew no one man could shovel them all clean.

But Hercules had a plan. He tore a huge opening in each wall of the cattle-yard. Then, he dug wide trenches to two rivers that flowed nearby.

The rivers rushed through the stables, flushing them out. Hercules had surprised everyone and finished his fifth Labor.

For his sixth Labor, Hercules was to drive away a flock of
giant, man-eating birds.

Hercules knew he couldn't fight thousands of birds. So, he
brought pair of bronze noisemaking clappers. Hercules used
all of his mighty strength and clashed the clappers together.

The noise was so loud it made the birds scared of men.
They fled far away from humankind, never to return.

The seventh Labor was easy for Hercules.

Hercules was to go to Crete and wrestle the Cretan Bull. This bull had run down many men who had tried to wrestle it.

When Hercules got to Crete, he easily wrestled the bull to the ground. Then, he took it back to King Eurystheus as a gift.

Eurystheus needed a more difficult challenge. So, he sent Hercules after the man-eating horses of Diomedes as his eighth Labor.

Hercules brought his mighty club and fought with the man-eaters for three days. Eventually, he defeated the Diomedian horses.

After his victory, Hercules put an iron bit in the mouth of each horse. He harnessed them to a chariot and drove them all the way back to Mycenea. This proved he had completed his eighth Labor.

For the ninth Labor, Eurystheus ordered Hercules to bring him the belt of Hippolyte.

Hippolyte was the queen of a tribe of warrior women known as Amazons. The belt was a gift from the war god Ares.

During the voyage to the Amazon's island, Hercules made a plan. Rather than trying to fight the Amazons, Hercules asked Hippolyte if he could borrow the belt.

Hippolyte wanted to help the hero and agreed to loan it to him.

The goddess Hera secretly watched nearby. Hera did not want Hercules to succeed in one more Labor.

Hera played a trick on the Amazons and Hercules. This trick got both sides to fight each other.

The battle lasted many nights. Hercules and his crew finally managed to flee the island with Hippolyte's belt.

Hercules had completed his ninth Labor.

For his final Labor, Eurystheus ordered Hercules to bring
him the cattle of the monster Geryon. Geryon had three
heads and three sets of legs all joined at the waist.

On his island, Geryon kept a herd of red cattle. The herd
was guarded by Orthus, a giant two-headed hound.

Hercules found the herd on the far side of the island. He hid, but Orthus smelled Hercules and attacked.

Hercules bashed at Orthus with his club. But Orthus bit it in two.

Hercules pounded with his fists, but it seemed to do no good. Finally, Hercules overpowered the mighty guard dog.

Hercules and his men quickly gathered up the herd.

Hercules had almost escaped with the cattle when Geryon attacked.

Hercules fought with the hideous beast. Meanwhile, his men loaded the last of the cattle on board their ship.

When the cattle were loaded, Hercules ordered his men to set sail.

Geryon and Hercules traded mighty blows as the ship got farther out to sea.

Hercules summoned all of the strength he had left. Finally, he defeated the mighty Geryon with a blow.

He then jumped into the ocean and swam as hard as he could. Hercules was happy to have finished the tenth and final Labor.

It had been eight years since Hercules set out on his ten Labors. He thought he had completed his punishment.

However, Eurystheus did not feel two of the Labors were completed properly. He demanded two more Labors from Hercules.

Hercules was angry, but he agreed to finish his punishment. Eurystheus next commanded Hercules to bring him Zeus's golden apples.

Hera had given these apples to Zeus as a wedding gift. They were protected and their location was a secret.

Eurytheus was certain Hercules could not finish this task. The golden apples were kept in a garden at the northern edge of the world.

They were guarded by the Hesperides and a hundred-headed dragon named Ladon. The Hesperides were nymphs and the daughters of Atlas. Hercules did not know where the garden was but he knew how to find it.

The sea-god Nereus knew the garden's secret location. Hercules found Nereus and didn't release him until he got the information he needed.

Hercules continued on his quest. He was stopped by Antaeus, the son of the sea god Poseidon, and was forced to fight him.

Hercules won and continued on his journey. He met and saved Prometheus from a terrible eagle. In his gratitude, Prometheus told Hercules how to steal the golden apples.

Using Prometheus's advice, Hercules set out to find Atlas.

Atlas was a titan forced to hold up the sky and the earth. He hated this and agreed to go and fetch the apples while Hercules took Atlas's place.

Hercules now stood with the weight of the world on his shoulders.

Atlas retrieved the apples and returned in no time.
But, now Atlas did not want to take back the sky and
the earth.

Hercules knew he had to trick Atlas. He told Atlas he
wanted to put some soft padding on his back before
Atlas left.

Atlas agreed and Hercules took advantage of this.
He snatched up the apples and fled back to Mycenea.
There, he gave the apples to Eurystheus, and fulfilled
his eleventh Labor.

Of all the Labors, the twelfth and final one was the most dangerous.

Eurystheus commanded Hercules to go to the Underworld. There, he was to kidnap the three-headed beast Cerberus.

Hercules proceeded cautiously. No mortal had ever returned from the Underworld.

Hercules attacked and threw his strong arms around the hound. He struggled to grasp all three heads at once.

There was a dragon in the tail of the fierce guard dog. This dragon bit Hercules. But that did not stop him.

Hercules was determined to end his punishment.

Hercules and Cerberus wrestled for days. Eventually,
Hercules beat the hound!

Hercules brought Cerberus to Eurystheus. Then, he announced he would never again be anyone's servant.

Hercules left Mycenea and returned Cerberus safely to Hades. Hercules then set out to create his own adventures.

They would make Hercules a legend on Earth and on Mount Olympus.